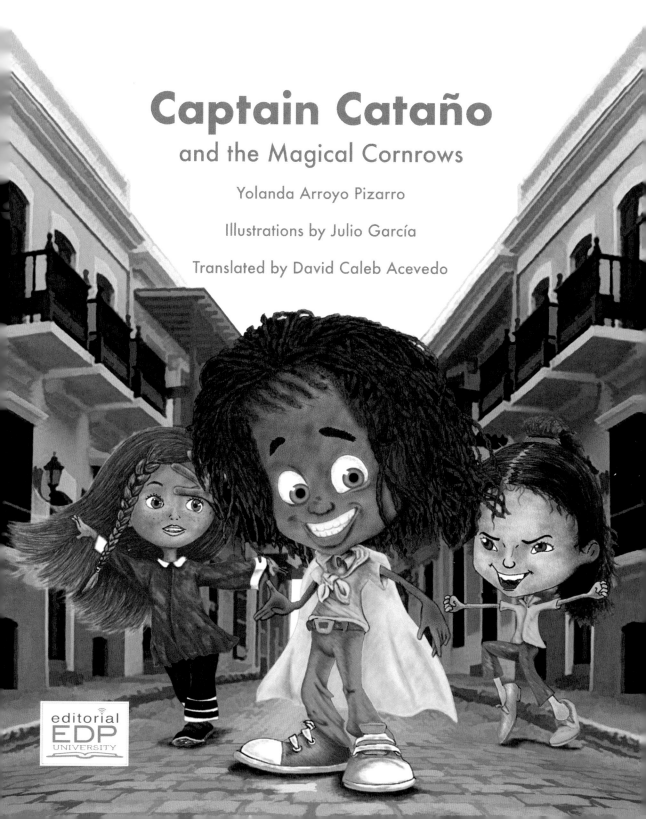

Captain Cataño
and the Magical Cornrows

Yolanda Arroyo Pizarro

Illustrations by Julio García

Translated by David Caleb Acevedo

editorial
EDP
UNIVERSITY

ISBN: 978-1-09-630003-8

Third Edition:2018

©Yolanda Arroyo Pizarro, 2015
©Editorial EDP University, 2015

Illustrations: Julio García

Editing and correction: Edgardo Machuca Torres
Design: Linnette Cubano García

This project is part of the work of the Chair of Ancestral Black Women directed by Yolanda Arroyo Pizarro as an initiative to celebrate the International Decade of African Descendants convened by UNESCO (2015–2024)

EDP University of Puerto Rico, Inc.
Ave. Ponce de León 560
Hato Rey, P.R.
PO Box 192303
San Juan, P.R. 00919-2303

www.edpuniversity.edu

 Editorial EDP

To Víctor Arroyo Pizarro

I ask the indulgence of the children for dedicating this book to a grownup. I have a serious reason: he is the best human being in the world. I have another reason: this grown-upunderstands everything, even books about children. I have a third reason: he grew up with me, in Barrio Amelia of Guaynabo, and on Cataño's streets. On one occasion, due to a car accident, he almost died and I suffered long and neverending nights singing to him, so that he didn't die, although he could not hear me. If all these reasons are not enough, I will dedicate this book to the child from whom this grown-up grew. All grown-ups were once children—although few of them remember it. And so I correct my dedication:

To Víctor Arroyo Pizarro, when he was a little boy.

Bright and unruly sun rays enter through the ample window brows of painter Ashanti Ayala's workshop. Each shimmer of light crosses the translucent sky and tops on the surfaces of the colourful atrium in the Cataño bay. The windows look like the broad eyes of the house, and its curtains, the lashes that hang in the breeze and which contrast with the watercolors in their wells, in the tubes of diverse combinations, in the mix residues left in the brushes. The fabrics, canvasses, and easels show hues that go from clear to dark, harmonizing the colors. Thus, the path glittered by the sun lands on the different paintings that are finished and ready for sale, and on those still unfinished, made by the virtuous watercolour artist, and which she places on the walls, tables, or floor. Some have price tags; others, a note that reads "Reserved" if it has been previously ordered by a customer.

Everything in the room is color and joy. Ashanti is an ever-smiling woman. Her eyes, curls, and cinnabar skin emphasise the festivity that can be breathed inside the house. From the door, one can see Isla de Cabras and San Felipe del Morro Castle. Both extremes of land are separated by a plain serving as a frontier; a calm sea opening, a salty distance that often brings together the two bodies of land, which are painted opaque gray by storm or rain. Only then, everything looks like a bunch of painting brushes, a piece of canvas itself, transmitting cold and warm hues, like a cosmos of colours.

Ashanti sings "*toco, toco, toco, toco*" while her hands create forms with the help of brushes and teasels.

2

"Mum, I want to cut my hair!" Eleven-year-old Viti demands in a shouting voice and decisive tone, while he barges in his mother's studio.

Ashanti stops what she was doing. She was about to give the finishing touches to a watercolor painting where a *vejigante* danced on the beach of the ferry town. She takes off her apron and steps away from the easel with great skill, even though she's on her wheelchair. She places the brushes and other tools on the table she uses daily in her studio. She observes her little son with a bit of humour and surprise, and smiles.

"Really? Explain that to me, Viti. I want to pay you all the attention in the world."

"Well, what I've told you, Mum. I want to cut my hair. It's already too long and high. Yesterday, my classmates made fun of me at school."

"They made fun of you?"

"Yes, Mum."

"Then, on Monday early in the morning I'll go talk to the school principal, so that she and your teacher talk to those children who make fun of you. It's very bad behavior that must be erradicated. But for now, come here. I want to tell you something important."

Ashanti, in her loving manner, brings the child close and caresses the afro she loves so much.

"I love you," she tells him. "Remember that we are all different, not just in our eye color, but also in our skin. And the texture of our hair. Yours, Viti, is beautiful."

"But it's too high," the boy insists.

"Have you forgotten what I told you once about the height of the afro?"

"No, Mum."

"Let's see... What did I tell you, Viti?"

Viti's face glows. A smile of pride takes over his mouth and he answers:

"You told me that the higher my afro, the more people of my past sleeps, rests, and lives in it. You told me that when my afro is big, I can keep my grandparents Víctor and Ramona in it. Also my great-grandparents Coco and Petronila, and my great-great-grandparents Miguelina and Ángel... And their brothers and cousins. And even their own grandparents, great-greandparents, and great-great-grandparents."

"Do you remember who where our grandparents, great-grandparents, and great-great-grandparents?"

"Yes," he exclaims in pure joy.

"Then tell me who..."

"*Cimarrones!*"

"Perfect! Brilliant."

"And *cimarrón* means..." Viti starts, but interrupts as he reaches with his hands for the palette of colors, brushes, and teasels that his mother has placed over the table. He touches the red color with his index and heart fingers, and draws lines of paint on both cheeks.

"So tell me. What does *cimarrón* mean?"

"*Cimarrón* is slave that was able to escape, like my ancestors, who escaped from their chains and went to live in the mountain, because they didn't want to get caught. They enjoyed being free."

"That's right. *Cimarrón* also means 'to want freedom.'"

"Freedom!" Viti shouts jubilant while he runs around his mother's studio.

Ashanti joins in and plays with him, also running around her studio on her wheelchair, driving it with great skill. Both shout, sing, and dance.

Then, she notices the time.

"My dear child, look at the clock! It'll soon be time for you to leave. Your sculpture class will start soon! The ferry must be about to arrive to port. You must go now."

Ashanti cleans Viti's face, so that he doesn't leave with red on his cheeks. It's Saturday, and like all Satudays, Viti must take the Cataño ferry to the other side of the bay, towards Old San Juan, to take a sculpture class at the Liga de Arte. Along with children, he observes the teacher's instructions to make clay sculptures.

Before Viti leaves, Ashanti reminds him:

"Viti, I just remembered that they said on the news that Paseo La Princesa in Old San Juan will be closed for construction works."

"Mum, that's the street I use to get to the Liga de Arte."

"Exactly. That's why I'm telling you. You must take another road when you step off the ferry. Take Tanca Street until the end. It will lead you straight to San Sebastián Street, and once there, take a left until you get to the Liga de Arte."

Viti's face saddens:

"I won't remember all that, Mum," he says. "Could you draw me a map?"

Ashanti gets an idea and tells him:

"I'll do you a better one. Bring me your comb and coconut oil. Make it a big-toothed comb."

Viti obeys. He looks for what his mother requested and comes back.

"Now, come here. Sit on my lap," Ashanti says.

Viti quickly jumps and sits, allowing his mother to brush and part his hair in order to braid it.

"I'm not too heavy, right, Mum?" the little boy asks worried.

"No, my darling. Remember that my legs can't feel anything."

"I want you to have new legs, Mum."

"Viti, I've told you already that that's not posible after the accident I had. And besides, I don't need them. I've got the best son in the world who helps me around with everything. I've got good neighbours, and your uncle Gabriel helps me a lot when he comes to visit. Besides, what have I told you about the soul of good people?"

"That good people who do good things have a free soul. Free!"

Ashanti cackles out loud.

"That's right. We good people are free in our hearts and minds. There's no need for legs, because I can walk and run all I want in my mind."

"Like the *cimarrones*, Mum. Free!"

"That's right!"

While Ashanti parts his hair, divides and pierces it with her comb and braids bunches of hair, intertwining them in order to join them, Viti remains quiet and asks her to tell him stories.

"Tell me about when you could walk, Mum. About when your legs were ok, before you jumped into the sea and accidentally hit your back with the rock."

Ashanti tells him of those *bomba y plena* parties in Loíza, when she was a *bailadora* and *tamborera* in the patron feasts procession of saints that took place in several towns. She tells him of when she used to dress up as *vejigante* in Piñones, of when she dressed as a *cabezudo* in the Feasts of San Sebastián and Hatillo. Viti loves listening to her and reviving her past through the stories she tells him.

He is so fascinated while learning details of Ashanti's past that he doesn't notice just how fast she finishes combing him. She

looks at him and smiles. Then says:

"Now go to the mirror."

Viti obeys. When he walks to the mirror, he notices that the afro on his head is gone. His hair is now a blooming jar of a dozen cornrows, beautifully designed all through his head.

"Awesome, Mum! It's been a while since I had cornrows! I was already missing them!"

"I've made them so they can guide you."

" How come?"

"So that you don't get lost on your way to the Liga de Arte in San Juan."

Ashanti places the tip of her finger on her son's forehead.

"That's your point of reference," she says. "Put your finger here."

The boy obeys. Then his mother remarks:

"Imagine that this is the ferry station in Old San Juan. If you walk straight, just as I marked your braids, this is how you'll get to Tanca Street. See?"

Viti traces the road with his fingers, discovering the braided map his Mum made in his cornrows.

"Yep. I get it. And when I get to that point, you made a cornrow on the left so I don't forget to turn there!"

"That's right, my love."

"And these knots like steps I feel here?"

"When you feel that, it means that you are in San Sebastián Street and those are the stairways that will lead you to the Liga de Arte."

"Then, I'll know I'm close."

"Exactly."

"Thanks, Mum."

Ashanti tells her son that, in the past, the hairstyles worn by *cimarrón* slaves marked the way towards the yearned land. After women came back from the fields, they combed braids close to the scalp of their daughters' and sons' hair, and used cornrows to draw the map that would guide them towards the escape route. This is how the slaves planned a very particular way, intertwined in their afros, of identifying the paths they traversed during the day. They would see the rivers, mountains, caves, and trails in the traces of their braids.

Viti bursts in applause once Ashanti finishes her story.

5

As Viti is about to leave, Ashanti gets a piece of yellow cloth with green sparkles from one of the chests in her art studio. The cloth has a very prominent letter "C" in it.

"Don't forget this, my son!"

"My superhero cape!", the boy screams with joy.

"Yes, my love. You're my superhero. My Captain Cataño!"

Like every Saturday, Viti walks proud along the coast of his hometown, his Captain Cataño cape tied to his neck and waving behind him. In his imagination, he was powers. He plays, runs, and jumps onto the waterfront while imagining himself in an enchanted place. The shore of Cataño offers remarkable treasures for him to find: blue land crabs, soldier crabs, small crabs, urchins, grasshoppers, and starfish. Viti pokes them with a small rod, runs after them so they dance with him, names them and smiles at them. On the road, he also encounters neighbours that greet him,

among which is Doña Paquita, a fisherwoman from the area, who hugs him and asks about his mother.

"She's okay, Doña Paquita. I'm off to my Saturday class. If you want, visit her and say hello."

"Thanks, Viti. God bless you, sweetheart."

Viti says hello to several other fishermen on their boats, to a *kioskito* cook who's frying *bacalaítos* and *alcapurrias* close to the beach, and to other kids from the neighbourhood that greet him with joy.

When he gets to the Cataño

6

ferry, he meets two classmates who also take the Saturday class with him at the Liga de Arte: Vanesa, red-haired, freckled with giant eye glasses, and Susie, a black girl with Caucasian traits and a pony tail full of curls. They greet each other, insert the coins in the turnstile, and board the ferry.

Captain Abraham greets them.

"'Ello, Vanesa. 'Ello, Susie," he exclaims, then adds: "'Ello, Captain Cataño."

The children greet him back with smiles on their faces. Captain Abraham is always kind to them, and, since he knows their parents from his days of youth, he takes care of them during the trip. When Captain Abraham and the children's parents were children, they all attended the same school in the coast town.

The three children climb up to the second floor of the ferry because they enjoy the wind blowing on their faces. The ferry is

blue, white and gray, and an orange strip stands out in the middle. The strip reminds Viti of one of his mother's paintings. She had painted a very beautiful canvas and hung it in his room. It portrays an organge smiling whale, which Ashanti once compared to the Cataño ferry. The first time Viti went on it on his way to Old San Juan, his mother asked him to imagine the ferry was a friendly whale that would take him there on its back. That's why every time Viti gets on the boat he's not afraid, but thinks he's riding on the humpback of a friendly whale.

The ferry cuts throught he ample sea that divides the two coast towns: Cataño and the capital city of the country, San Juan. The waves lash against the vessel, which goes along with several dolphins that jump out of the water as if saying hi. From time to time, the splashes of salty water drop on the high-spirited faces of Viti, Susie, and Vanesa.

The children count the amount of dolphins they see on the silver ocean. Captain Cataño is very interested in his cape with the letter "C", which waves violently on the wind until they get to the other shore and leave the port.

"Oh, oh," Susie says. "The main entrance is closed. We must take the side exit."

Indeed, the front entrance was closed and a sign announces that due to construction works, the lateral exit is the one they must take in order to exit.

"Don't worry," Viti says. "My Mum had already told me that we were going to have to take another route. She drew it in my cornrows."

Susie and Vanesa follow him without understanding much of his words. When they exit the new wooden path they take, Viti notices that they end up on another road that doesn't lead to Tanca Street.

"Damn, I didn't expect this," they boy exclaims.

"Now what? Do we ask for directions?" Vanesa asks.

Captain Cataño thinks for a while, then make a decision:

"We'll read the streetsigns to know our location."

7

They walk a bit and they find the name of the cobblestoned path: San Justo Street. Captain Cataño beckons his friends to follow him so that they don't get lost. They arrive to the corner, where a *piragüero* sells the island's folkloric iced beverages *piragüas* with tamarind, cream, strawberry, and coconut-flavoured syrups.

Viti asks the *piragüero* how close are they to Tanca Street. He tells them that San Justo Street, where they are, runs parallel to Tanca Street.

"What does 'parallel' mean?" Viti asks, whose mother has taught him never to be afraid of asking something if he doesn't know what it means. "Wise men always ask," Ashanti told him then, and Viti has never forgotten those words.

"Parallel means that they run one besides the other one, together, like my two arms, without crossing each other."

"So they lead to the same place," Vanesa exclaims.

"Exactly," the *piragüero* responds.

"So, ff they are parallel, we can take that street and it will lead us directly to..." Viti starts, but gets confused. He suddenly says: "Susie, could you touch my cornrows to see where it will lead us?"

"Your cornrows?" she asks surprised.

"Mum made a map that leads to the Liga de Arte in my cornrows."

With some doubt, Susie traces Viti's rows of braids from the forehead, like he asks. At the part that turns to the left, the boy exclaims:

"I just remembered! We make a left on San Sebastián Street."

"That's precisely right," the *piragüero* says. "Almost towards the end of San Justo Street, you'll find San Sebastián, where the famous feasts take place, and you turn there."

"Thank you very much," the children say at the same time and they leave.

They walk on the cobblestones that seem like a mountain that must be ascended, because the slope climbs upwards. First, they play at who gets to the corner first, and they encounter Fortaleza Street, and Viti wins. Then they play at who gets first to the other corner, always ascending and running, and Susie wins and screams:

"This is the corner of San Francisco Street!"

They run again and Vanesa wins, pointing to a beautiful house at the corner of Luna Street, with colonial windows that show a birdcage with two macaws. The birds greet them, "Hello, hello!", and the three kids answer with another "Hello, hello!"

At the next corner, Sol Street, there's a seller of local ice cream. "Coconut! Pineapple!" he announces. The children decide to buy one and divide it between all of them. The ice cream man is very kind to them and asks Viti what does the "C" in his cape stands for.

"I'm a superhero. I'm Captain Cataño," the boy answers.

"And what's his superpower?" the ice cream man asks.

Susie answers:

"His superpower is his cornrows. They become a map that doesn't let us get lost. Ha, ha, ha."

"Is that so? That's nice. That's what our ancestors used to do," the man says.

"Yes," Viti confirms. "My Mum told me. *Cimarrón* slaves did them so they didn't get lost when escaping to their freedom."

"Exactly. How nice that your Mum tells you these beautiful stories. Thank her on my behalf."

"I will!" Viti shouts, already running uphill. He is the first to arrive at the next corner.

"San Sebastián!"

At the corner of San Sebastián Street there's a man to plays the congas with great skill and agility. Ashanti has told her son that those drums come from Africa and that it is a great privilege to play them. The *conguero* uses the palms of his hands and the elbows to produce rhythmic sounds from the leather lids of each drum. The kids watch as several dancers approach to dance to the rhythm of the congas. The bailadoras start a game with their skirts and the sound played by the conguero.

Viti, Susie, and Vanesa applaud and run, turning to the left.

Then, they find the Liga de Arte building and sit in front of the stairways to catch their breaths.

"Your Mum had a great idea. Next Saturday I'll ask mine to make me cornrows too," Susie says.

"I'll also ask to have my hair braided," Vanesa adds. "We've had so much fun. And all thanks to your magic cornrows!"

Viti remains silent, but smiles and watches the sea far away from

where he's seating. The cape with the "C" waves in the wind. He thinks of how fortunate he is to have a mother like Ashanti, and of how beautiful are his island, his Old San Juan, and his beloved Cataño.

Paint
Captain Cataño

Yolanda Arroyo-Pizarro is the Puerto Rican writer who loves *The Little Prince* the most. She has a collection of over 220 copies in several sizes and languages, such as Japanese, Greek, Turkish, Italian, Nahuatl, and Braille. Her stories are populated by stars, planets, and asteroids, a clear homage to the novel that holds so much meaning to her. The author is the mother of a beautiful daughter, Aurora, who has also been her inspiration for many of her poems, short stories, and novels. The author's virtual blog is entitled *Boreales*, and has been enticed by the same boreal and austral lights that can be seen from the North and South Poles, as well as a clear homage to her only daughter.

Her work promotes amazing lessons of social justice and equality among all human beings. It also renders visible her impassioned approaches to the discussion of the African identity and the eradication of racism. She is the Director of the Department of African Puerto Rican Studies, a creative writing performance project that responds to the call made by UNESCO of celebrating the International Decade for People of African Descent. She directs the *Cátedra de Mujeres Negras Ancestrales* [Ancestral Black Women Scholarship] with seat at EDP University in San Juan, Puerto Rico, and has been invited by the United Nations to the Program

"Remembering Slavery" to talk about women, slavery, and creativity in 2015, and to present the Cátedra Project in Harvard University in 2017.

This activist who loves writing on the boats of her native Cataño, has won the following awards: Premio Nacional del Instituto de Cultura Puertorriqueña in 2008, Premio Nacional de Cuento PEN Club de Puerto Rico in 2013, and Premio del Instituto de Cultura Puertorriqueña in 2012 and 2015. She was selected as one of the most important writers in Latin America in 2007 during the Bogotá39 initiative and was selected as Writer of the Year in Puerto Rico in 2016.

She has published the children and young adult books: *Thiago y la aventura del huracán* (Editorial EDP University, 2018), *Las Reyas Magas* (Editorial EDP University, 2017), *Negrita linda como yo: versos dedicados a la vida de la Maestra Celestina Cordero* (Cátedra de Mujeres Ancestrales, 2017); *Oscarita: la niña que quiere ser como Óscar López Rivera* (Cátedra de Mujeres Ancestrales, 2016), *María Calabó* (Cátedra de Mujeres Ancestrales, 2016), *Las caras lindas* (Editorial EDP University, 2016), *Capitán Cataño y las trenzas mágicas* (Editorial EDP University, 2015), *Thiago y la aventura de los túneles de San Germán* (Editorial EDP University, 2015), *Mis dos mamás me miman* (Editorial Boreales, 2011), and *La linda señora tortuga* (Ediciones Santillana, 2017). Yolanda loves to read, write, dance and singing off key. During her adolescence, she used to paint and draw, and she would love to connect again with that art. She is a fan of the Eiffel Tower, domino, and dark chocolate.

Made in the USA
Middletown, DE
29 April 2022

65002099R00024